# Bertie Wiggins' Amazing Ears

## DAVID COX and ERICA JAMES

### Illustrated by Pat McCarthy

Oxford University Press

# OXFORD
UNIVERSITY PRESS

Great Clarendon Street, Oxford OX2 6DP

Oxford University Press is a department of the University of Oxford.
It furthers the University's objective of excellence in research, scholarship,
and education by publishing worldwide in

Oxford New York

Auckland Bangkok Buenos Aires Cape Town Chennai
Dar es Salaam Delhi Hong Kong Istanbul Karachi Kolkata
Kuala Lumpur Madrid Melbourne Mexico City Mumbai
Nairobi São Paulo Shanghai Taipei Tokyo Toronto

Oxford is a registered trade mark of Oxford University Press
in the UK and in certain other countries

Database right Oxford University Press (maker)

First published 1995

10

ISBN 0 19 916868 7

Printed in China

Illustrations by Pat McCarthy c/o J Martin & Artists Ltd.

# As clever as Prince Cecil

'Five times five!' said Mrs Lines.

She had a way of saying things softly that sounded as if she was shouting at you.

Everyone in the class wrote something down, except Bertie.

Bertie chewed on the end of his pencil. What was the answer? He wished he could work it out. But he couldn't.

The trouble was, Bertie was no good at sums. No matter how hard he tried, he couldn't remember past his three times table.

He felt his ears beginning to twitch again.

Sadie Smith looked at Bertie and started to smile.

Mrs Lines looked up and said, sharply, 'Sadie! What is the matter?'

THE SPACE
SCUTTLE

Sadie blushed. 'Nothing, Mrs Lines,' she said. But Mrs Lines could see for herself that Bertie's ears were wiggling. The trouble was, Bertie's ears didn't wiggle just a little bit. They wiggled and waggled as if they were waving at you.

'Bertie Wiggins!' she said. 'Stop that at once. If you spent as much time on your work as you spend twitching your ears, you'd be as clever as Prince Cecil.'

Everyone in the class grinned. They all knew that Bertie looked a bit like Prince Cecil.

Bertie sighed. He was fed up with jokes about looking like a prince.

'I hope you are all going to watch Prince Cecil this evening,' said Mrs Lines.

Everyone knew how clever Prince Cecil
was. Prince Cecil was very good at sums.
Prince Cecil knew his tables.

Every year the King went on television and
one of his children went on with him. Last
year it was Princess Maude playing her
trombone.

This year it was going to be Prince Cecil saying his tables.

A huge crowd went to the royal television show. Every year at the end, the crowd had to clap and cheer. Then the King made a big speech. He always began, 'Cleverness shows in many ways. It is most wonderful when it shows in someone young. The royal children ... '

Every time the royal children were on television, Bertie's mum and dad would moan at Bertie. 'You may look like Prince Cecil,' they would say, 'but you'll never get on television by flapping your ears.'

That afternoon Bertie had his tea and started doing his homework. After a few minutes, he gave up and turned on the television. A lady was speaking. 'Tonight, everyone must see Prince Cecil.' Bertie turned the television off.

He went outside and sat on the doorstep.
From next door he could hear music playing
on the radio. Bertie began to wiggle his ears.
First the left one. Then the right one. In no
time at all both ears were wiggling
backwards and forwards in time to the music.

Mrs Green from next door came past.
'That's good, Bertie,' she cried. 'You're a real
little act, you are.'

'No one else seems to think so,' grumbled
Bertie.

# The secret search

Just then, a car drove slowly into Bertie's street. It stopped right outside Bertie's house. A man and a woman got out. The man had a photo. To Bertie's surprise, they walked over to him.

The man looked at Bertie. Then he looked at the photo. 'It's amazing,' he said.

Bertie's mum and dad came outside.
'What's going on?' asked Mr Wiggins.

'We are from the Royal Palace,' said the
woman. 'Prince Cecil has got red spots. It
could be chicken pox. He can't be on the
royal television show this evening. The King
has ordered a secret search for a Prince Cecil
look-alike.'

She pulled out a crown and put it on
Bertie's head. The man held up the photo.

Mrs Wiggins gasped. 'It's our Bertie,' she cried.

'No, it's not,' said the man. 'It's Prince Cecil. We need your lad to take Prince Cecil's place on the show tonight.'

Mr Wiggins opened his mouth. Then he closed it again. At last he said, 'On television? Our Bertie? So we'll all be famous!'

'No you won't,' snapped the woman. 'No one will ever know. When Bertie goes on television this evening, everyone must think *he* is the prince. It's a secret you'll have to keep for ever.'

'Will we meet the King and Queen?' said Bertie's mum.

'Will there be a reward?' said Bertie's dad.

'Maybe,' said the man. 'But now we must get Bertie to the television studio.'

Bertie felt his blood run cold. Wasn't Prince Cecil going on television to do sums and say his tables? Bertie couldn't even get past his three times table. And as for sums … 'But Mum! But Dad!' said Bertie. It was no good. Nobody would listen.

Before Bertie could say any more, he was in the car with his mum and dad. They were on their way.

Bertie sat in the back of the car. He was
very worried. How could he pretend to be
Prince Cecil?

'We will go to the television studio now,'
said the woman. 'Bertie has to get ready. And
we must do something about his ears.'

At last Bertie gasped, 'But Prince Cecil is
supposed to show how clever he is. He's
supposed to say his tables. I can't do that!'

The woman sniffed. 'You don't have to be clever. All the answers will be on a screen in front of you.' She stared at him. 'You can read, can't you?'

'Of course I can,' said Bertie.

'Good,' she went on. 'No one else will be able to see the screen. No one will know that you can't do your tables.'

The King was pacing up and down in the television studio. 'I will not wait any longer!' he shouted. 'They must have found someone who looks like Cecil by now.'

At that moment, Mr and Mrs Wiggins arrived with Bertie.

Mr Wiggins bowed. 'This is Bertie,' he said. 'I'm glad we can help out, Your Majesty.'

The King looked at Bertie. He smiled. 'It's amazing,' he said. 'You could be Cecil, apart from the ears. Put Cecil's crown on and hide your ears.'

'But Your Majesty,' said Bertie. 'I am not Prince Cecil. I don't want to pretend to be him.'

'Nonsense,' said the King. 'You look like him. That's all that matters. Just do what you're told and read what's on the screen.'

It was time for the show to start. The people were in their seats. Bertie sat on a large chair. Music played. Then a man with a big smile spoke into the camera. 'Good evening, everyone. Tonight we are happy to welcome our young prince on the show. Prince Cecil is going to say his eight times table. What a clever lad!'

GOOD
EVENING
EVERYONE
TONIGHT
WE ARE
HAPPY TO

Autocue

Autocue

Lights shone on Bertie. A lady with headphones counted up to five on her fingers. A voice in his ear said, 'Now – ' And Bertie was on television.

Bertie felt his heart beating. He looked for the screen with the answers. There it was in front of him. He coughed, and began to read. 'One times eight is eight,' he said loudly.

Then the screen went blank.

# Bertie adds it up

Bertie's tummy felt as if it had insects buzzing around inside. He wanted to be sick. He knew what came next so he gasped, 'Two times eight is sixteen.' What was three times eight?

His ears began to twitch. Prince Cecil's crown wobbled from side to side. Bertie felt the crown slip over his eyes in little jerks.

He took the crown off. This seemed to stop his ears twitching.

Then the man spoke again. He did not sound so happy now. 'Well, Prince Cecil, what are three times eight?'

Bertie tried to count the answer out on his fingers. He took off his shoes and socks and counted his toes as well. But it was no good. He just didn't have enough fingers and toes.

One or two people called out, 'Come on! What are three times eight?' Bertie felt awful. He wanted to shout, 'I'm not Prince Cecil. I'm Bertie Wiggins.' But he couldn't say a word.

Then something strange happened. Bertie's ears began to move again. They slowly flapped back and forwards.

The crowd began to count along. 'One… two … three ….' The ears flapped twenty-four times, which is exactly three times eight.

Someone shouted, 'What about four times eight?'

The ears wiggled thirty-two times.

'His ears have got it right!' cried two ladies in the front row. The crowd cheered.

By the time Bertie's ears had counted out ten times eight, the crowd were jumping up and down with excitement.

The man looked at the King. He looked at Bertie. He didn't know what to do. 'Er ... Thank you, Prince Cecil ... um .... Or should I say, "Thanks to Prince Cecil's ears?"'

Everyone laughed, but the King scowled. 'Now the prince will do sums,' he shouted.

'Stop it, Dad!' cried a voice.

Two children darted across the studio. One
was Princess Maude. The other was the real
Prince Cecil. Now there were two Prince Cecils
in front of the camera.

Princess Maude pointed at Bertie. 'This is
not Prince Cecil,' she said.

'No, I'm Bertie Wiggins,' said Bertie.

Everyone gasped. The King went red in the
face. Mrs Wiggins fainted.

Princess Maude went on, 'Prince Cecil is not very good at sums. He hates going on television. We both do. Last year I had to pretend to play the trombone. I can't really play it at all.'

By now the King had jumped to his feet. He began to roar, 'Stop the show! Cecil! You should be in bed with spots. Maude! Be quiet!'

But Princess Maude took no notice. 'I
painted Cecil with red spots.'

'You!' cried the King.

'Yes,' said Prince Cecil. 'But we didn't think
you would find someone who looks like me.'

'So we came here by taxi,' went on Princess
Maude. 'We had to stop this stupid show. We
hate it because it makes everyone laugh at
us. They think we're too good to be true.'

The King put his head in his hands.

'But we have always gone on the royal television show. That's what it's for.'

'Yes,' said the man. He did not look happy at all. 'What about my show?'

'I know,' said Bertie bravely. 'Why don't you put on a show that children will really like? Children from all over the country could go on it.'

'Wow! Talent spotting,' said Prince Cecil.
'What a good idea.'

'Go on, Dad,' said Princess Maude. 'Say
yes.'

The King went white and then he went red.
Then he went purple. But everyone in the
studio began to clap and cheer.

'Well … all right,' he said. 'But my children
must tell everyone what to do.'

'No, Dad,' said Prince Cecil. 'We never want to show off again.'

'Then Bertie can do all his tables,' boomed the King. 'And he can teach everyone sums with his ears.'

Prince Cecil and Princess Maude groaned.

'No sums, thank you,' said Bertie. Then he grinned. He was enjoying himself on television. He wiggled his ears. 'But you wait. One day I'll really be the star of the show.'

TV TIMES MONDAY

6·00 am
RISE WITH BW

7:00 am
BREAKFAST NEWS

8:00 am
BERTIE'S WEATHER CHART

8:10
MORE NEWS

.00
CHILDRENS PROGRAMMES

BERTIE WIGGINS AND HIS AMAZING EARS

MONDAY    TV TIMES

6·00
BERTIES HOUSE PARTY

7:30
EAR WATCH

8:00
WIGGINS WORLD

9:00
FROM EAR TO THERE AND BACK TO EAR

10:00
EAR WATCH

10:30
YET MORE NEWS

EARS LOOKIN AT YOU KID

BERTIE WIGGINS TONIGHTS FILMS

DIRTY BERTIE

# About the author

I was born in London in 1963, the youngest of seven children. At least twice a day I see something worth writing about.

Once I saw an elephant pushing a shopping trolley around a supermarket car park. I really did. The poor elephant had run away from a circus. I didn't know this at the time and I thought he was looking for his car. Perhaps in a story he could have been?

In case you are wondering, Erica James is not her real name. It is a pen name for a well-known children's writer.

**Other Treetops books at this level include:**

*Flans Across the River* by Nick Warburton
*Hard to Please* by Nick Warburton
*Coming Clean* by Nick Warburton
*Bertha's Secret Battle* by John Coldwell
*Amy the Hedgehog Girl* by John Coldwell

**Also available in packs**

| | |
|---|---|
| *Stage 11 pack A* | 0 19 916871 7 |
| *Stage 11 class pack A* | 0 19 916872 5 |